S0-BON-689

A DAY AT
THE ZOO

BY MARION CONGER

PICTURES BY
TIBOR GERGELY

SIMON AND SCHUSTER • NEW YORK

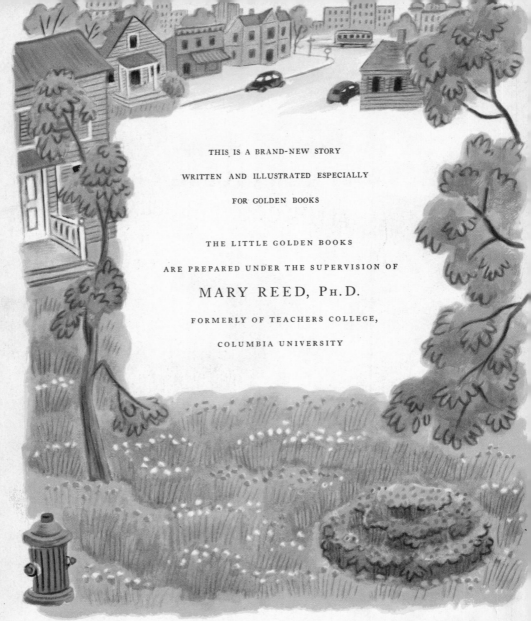

THIS IS A BRAND-NEW STORY

WRITTEN AND ILLUSTRATED ESPECIALLY

FOR GOLDEN BOOKS

THE LITTLE GOLDEN BOOKS

ARE PREPARED UNDER THE SUPERVISION OF

MARY REED, Ph.D.

FORMERLY OF TEACHERS COLLEGE,

COLUMBIA UNIVERSITY

It is summertime. There are new leaves on the trees, new flowers in the grass. At the zoo there are new baby animals. Molly and her Daddy are going to see them.

"Don't hurry home," says Molly's Mother.
"There is so much to see at the zoo."

Molly and her Daddy leave their car outside the
zoo and walk through the great iron gates.

There are so many paths they can't decide which to take. Molly closes her eyes and spins around three times. When she opens them, she sees a sign that says TO THE LIONS AND TIGERS.

So they go to see the lions and tigers first. The
lioness lies in her cage watching her cubs. They are
soft and sleepy. Molly would like to cuddle them.

The lion paces back and forth.

"I am the king of the beasts!" he roars. "I am the father of these beautiful babies!"

The tigers, too, pace back and forth. They are

big and strong, but they step as lightly as dancers.

The polar bear has a little snowball of a baby.
It tumbles along the rocks after its mother.

And—KERSPLASH—the two bears dive into their icy pool.

Now Molly and her Daddy want to feed the deer. So they buy some animal food.

The baby deer are gentle and friendly. What slender legs they have! What big eyes!

One of them is bolder than the rest. He lets
Molly feed him.

Molly laughs when his slippery nose tickles
her hand.

The hippopotamus is yawning lazily. His mouth opens wider and wider and WIDER AND WIDER. There was never such an enormous yawn.

Next come the riding rings. Molly sees a boy riding a pony and a girl riding a donkey and some children riding a llama cart.

Then she sees the camels. Some of them have howdahs on their backs, and the keeper lifts Molly onto a howdah.

Away she goes round the camel pen. HUMPETY
BUMPETY BUMPETY HUMP. Molly's heart goes
THUMPETY THUMP.

The camel ride makes Molly hungry. So she and
her Daddy have lunch at a little table under a striped
umbrella. They have hot dogs in buns and frosty
chocolate milks.

In front of them is the sea lion pool. The baby
sea lions race the big sea lions through the water.
Their wet black coats gleam in the sun.

When a man comes with a fish basket, they bark
loudly. He throws the fish. And the sea lions catch
them, every one.

Molly and her Daddy buy ice cream cones for dessert and walk away licking them. Up and down the paths they go.

Beside one path are the gayest birds Molly has ever seen. Red and blue and yellow birds. Pink and white and purple.

"Hello!" says a green parrot, "Polly wants a cracker!"

"Oh dear," says Molly, "I haven't any crackers."

"What's that? What's that?" asks the parrot.

Molly would like to talk longer with the parrot, but there is still a lot to see.

Molly and her Daddy see the giraffe. But will he
let Molly feed him? No, his neck is too long. He
nibbles green leaves high in the trees.

Molly sees a baby kangaroo peeking out of
its mother's pouch. HOPPITY WHOOSH. The
mother gives her baby a ride.

Molly sees a great gray elephant

and some small striped zebras.

She sees gruff old alligators

and two proud American eagles.

She sees aoudads and elands and kudus

and kinkajous and raccoons.

Then they came to the monkey house.

A chimpanzee jumps up and down and shakes the bars of his cage when he sees Molly. He is not fierce. He is just showing off.

Hundreds of monkeys are doing tricks.
The monkeys shriek and chatter. But quietly, in a quiet corner, a mother monkey rocks her baby on a swaying trapeze.

Molly and her Daddy have saved the children's
zoo till last. It is like a story book come alive.

They see the Three Little Pigs and Heidi and her
Kids and the Old Woman in a Shoe.

Baa Baa Black Sheep is there too. He is just a
baby black sheep. Molly feeds him milk from a
bottle with a nipple.

She makes a wish on the Wishing Seat.

And then they came to Noah's Ark. A boy who is just coming out of the Ark says there are MONSTERS inside.

Molly wants her Daddy to take her in. But a sign says "No Grown-ups Allowed." So she goes in alone, feeling shivery.

In the Ark was a mouse village
with its own houses and stores,
and even a make-believe theater.

She comes out smiling.
"Did you see the monsters?" asks her Daddy.
"Yes!" laughs Molly. "They were mice!"

Soon the iron gates will close. The animals will curl up in their pens and pits and cages to sleep.

As they drive home, a new moon silvers the sky and the first star twinkles at its tip. Molly wishes on them both.

"Will it spoil my wish to tell?" asks Molly.

"Not if you just tell me," says her Daddy.

"I wished to go to the zoo again," says Molly.

"That is a good wish," says her Daddy. "It will surely come true."

A DAY AT THE ZOO

Words and Music by Ethel Crowninshield

Evenly

Give me your hand and off we'll go,
See all the paths go up and down.

It's not far to the Zoo, you know.
Cag - es, cag - es, are all a - round.

Hur - ry up! Hur - ry up! I can't wait!
An - i - mals, an - i - mals, ev 'ry - where.

Here we go through the great big gate!
Not too close! Oh, take care, take care!

Now we will play a brand-new game,
Do you know every one by name?
There will be some that we know quite well,
There are some we could never tell!

Here is my wish and one for you,
Lots of things we can see and do.
Wishing my wishes will all come true!
Lots more days at the great big Zoo.